THE TALE OF MESHKA THE KVETCH

by Carol Chapman pictures by Arnold Lobel

E. P. DUTTON NEW YORK

A version of the text in this book first appeared
in *Cricket* magazine, March 1978, volume 5, number 7.

Library of Congress number 80-11225
ISBN 0-525-44494-7

Published in the United States by
E. P. Dutton, New York, N.Y.,
a division of Penguin Books USA Inc.

Published simultaneously in Canada by
Fitzhenry & Whiteside Limited, Toronto

Editor: Ann Durell   Designer: Riki Levinson

Printed in Hong Kong   First Unicorn Edition 1989
10 9 8 7 6 5 4 3 2 1

to Gloria Miklowitz,
my teacher

In the small village of Hemer lived Meshka, who was considered by all to be the village kvetch. Now *kvetch* is a Yiddish word for *complainer*, and that's just what Meshka did. Complain. From morning till night, nothing was right.

When the baker would ask her how she was feeling, Meshka would say, "Oy vey. My back, it feels as if I've carried the Wall of Jericho itself. And my feet! Let me tell you, they are swollen to the size of melons!"

Then the baker would shake his head from side to side.

When the dressmaker would ask how her children were, Meshka would say, "Oy vey. My son, he does nothing but read and sit around the house like a bump on a kosher pickle. And my daughter! She only visits me once a month. It's as if I don't exist the other twenty-nine days."

Then the dressmaker would shake her head from side to side.

And when the rabbi would ask Meshka how her home was, Meshka would say, "Oy vey. If only it were a home! But it's more like a box. Why my late husband couldn't have built a larger house, I'll never know."

Then the rabbi would shake his head from side to side.

And so it would go. No matter who was listening, Meshka had something to complain about.

Now on one particular morning, Meshka woke up and looked to the heavens and said, "If only I can have the strength to bear another miserable day!"

And as she spoke, her tongue itched. Not an ordinary itch, but a weird, tingly kind of itch.

"What is this itch?" said Meshka, crossing her eyes and trying to look at her tongue.

She could see nothing unusual, so she went into the kitchen and prepared breakfast. Then she called her son, but he did not come.

"Such a lazy boy!" said Meshka. "Like a bump on a kosher pickle."

Meshka went to her son's room. He was nowhere to be seen. But there on his bed was a huge, green pickle with one big bump on it. Meshka gasped at the sight. Then she searched the house for her son, but she could not find him.

"Where could he be in this little box of a house?" Meshka wondered aloud. And at that, her house groaned and creaked and began to shrink. Soon it was so small that Meshka's head was poking out the front door, and her legs were sticking out the windows.

Meshka was frantic, but she screamed and kicked until she had wiggled free.

"I've got to see my daughter and tell her of these strange things," panted Meshka as she ran through the village. "*If* she remembers her mama," she added.

When she reached her daughter's home, she knocked on the door.

"Yes, what is it, old woman?" said her daughter, opening the door.

"What is 'old woman'?" asked Meshka. "I'm your mama."

"You're not my mama," said her daughter. And she closed the door firmly.

Meshka was dumbfounded. "What is happening?" she exclaimed, clutching at her heart. "Isn't it enough that I am not well, that my back aches as if I were carrying the Wall of Jericho itself, that my feet are swollen like melons?"

At those words, Meshka's feet became ten-pound melons.

She lost her balance and rolled to the ground.

As she fell, a huge wall appeared, pinning her down.

And there she lay for a good hour, moaning over her dilemma.

Suddenly Meshka heard a voice. "And how is your home?"

Meshka looked up and saw the rabbi smiling down at her. "Oh, Rabbi," cried Meshka. "Let me tell you what has happened."

The rabbi listened as Meshka told him of her latest troubles.

When she had finished, the rabbi shook his head from side to side. "I have heard of such cases," he said. "Did your tongue itch a strange kind of itch this morning?"

"Yes, yes," Meshka exclaimed.

The rabbi shook his head again. "I'm afraid you have the Kvetch's Itch."

"The what?" asked Meshka.

"The Kvetch's Itch," repeated the rabbi. "It happens rarely, and only to a kvetch, and it causes everything the kvetch complains about to come true."

"Oy vey," cried Meshka. "I have caused these things to happen with my own words? How can this itch be cured?"

"It cannot be," said the rabbi. "You will have it the rest of your life."

At hearing this, Meshka let out a mournful wail.

"However," said the rabbi, raising a finger, "if you praise the good in your life, these problems you mention will cease."

Meshka frowned, thinking about what the rabbi had said. She didn't quite know how to praise, because she had never done it before. "Very well, Rabbi," said Meshka. "I will try." She cleared her throat and began. "My son who is lazy—"

"No, no," said the rabbi quickly. "*Praise* your son."

So Meshka started again. "My son who is good—"

"Yes, yes," cried the rabbi. "Go on."

"He reads to seek knowledge," continued Meshka. "My house is snug and well built. I am lucky that my daughter, who is busy with her own family, visits me once a month. I am grateful that I am living and in good health for a woman of my years."

At these words, the wall disappeared.

Meshka's feet became feet again. And Meshka's daughter opened the door of her house.

"Mama," she said. "I was just coming to visit you."

When Meshka returned to her home, she found it just as her husband had built it. And when she went into her son's room, there he was, reading a book and smelling a bit like pickle juice.

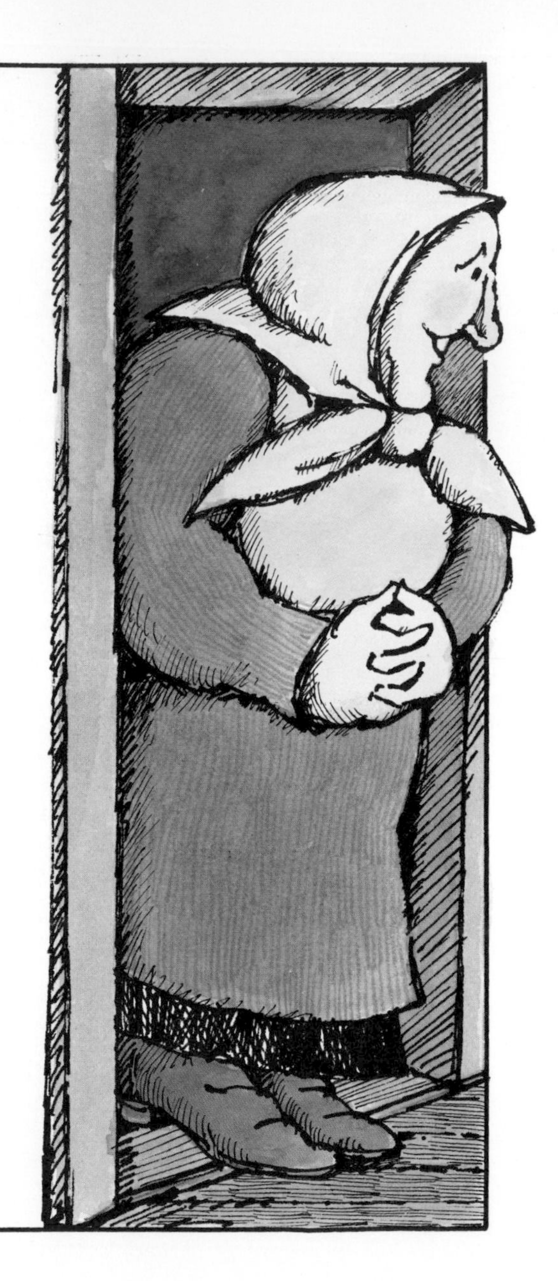

And from that day on, whenever Meshka would start to complain and say, "Oy vey—" she quickly said instead, "Things are good and I am happy."

And soon she was.